ANOTHER NATION

By the same author:

Poetry
Stalingrad: The Street Dictionary,
                            Raven Arts, 1980.
Atlantic Blues, *Raven Arts, 1982.*
The Diary of a Silence, *Raven Arts, 1985.*

Criticism
Patrick Kavanagh & the discourse of contemporary Irish poetry. *Raven Arts, 1985.*

Fiction
The Inside Story, *Raven Arts, 1989.*

Translation
Hidden Weddings – The Selected Poems of Gerrit Achterberg (from the Dutch)
                            Raven Arts, 1986.

ANOTHER NATION

New & Selected Poems

Michael O'Loughlin

1996

Published in the U.K. by
Arc Publications
Nanholme Mill, Shaw Wood Road
Todmorden, Lancs. OL14 6DA

Published in Ireland by
New Island Books
2 Brookside, Dundrum Road,
Dundrum, Dublin 14

Copyright © Michael O'Loughlin 1996

Printed by Arc & Throstle Press Ltd.
Nanholme Mill, Todmorden, Lancs.

ISBN 0 946407 75 4 (U.K.)
ISBN 1 874597 03 0 (Ireland)

Some of the poems in this volume have been previously published in *Stalingrad: The Street Dictionary, Atlantic Blues* and *The Diary of a Silence*. (Raven Arts 1980, 1982, 1985). The Irish Times, Kino, The Irish Review, Poetry Seeland Review, Maatstaf (Amsterdam) Stet, The Great Book of Ireland, RTE Radio.

Arc Publications acknowledge financial assistance from Yorkshire and Humberside Arts Board.

New Island Books receive financial assistance from The Arts Council (An Chomhairle Ealaíon), Dublin, Ireland.

Contents

I
The City / 9
Yellow / 10
Mandelstam / 11
The Journey / 12
Cuchulainn / 13
Babel / 14
Copenhagen Dreaming of Leningrad / 15
Hamlet in Dublin / 16
Boxer / 17
The Fugitive / 18
Two Women / 20

II
An Irish Requiem / 21

III
The Shards
  1. The Bunkers / 24
  2. The Birds / 25
  3. Frank Ryan Dead in Dresden! / 26
  4. From a Diary / 27
  5. Heinrich Böll in Ireland / 28
  6. Concert-going in Vienna / 29
  7. The Boys of '69 / 30
  8. The Shards / 31

IV
In the Suburbs
  1. A Letter To Marina Tsetaeva / 34
  2. The Music Lesson / 35
  3. In the Suburbs / 36
  4. The Knot / 37
From a Café / 38
On Board / 39
In a Bathroom / 40
The Chord / 41
Posthumous / 42

V

The Diary of a Silence / 44
Two Poems For Paddy Graham
   1. Summer in Monaghan / 46
   2. Heimat / 47
Three Fragments on the Theme of Moving Around in Cities
   I. Epitaph for Matt Talbot / 48
   II. Little Suburban Ode / 48
   III. Berlin / 48
One Version of a Myth / 49
Sea Fishing / 51
Intensity, Exaltation / 52
Elegy for the Unknown Soldier / 53
The East Wind / 54
The Black Piano / 55
Valparaiso / 56
Anne Frank / 58
Exiles / 59
On Hearing Michael Hartnett / 60
The Real Thing / 61
Latin as a Foreign Language / 62

VI

Glasnevin Cemetery / 65
Cigarette Elegy / 67
The Song of the Earth: Epitaph for a Dubliner of the 50s / 68
Night in the Suburbs of Dublin / 69
A Protestant Graveyard in County Monaghan / 70
At the Grave of Father Hopkins / 71
Words on an Ancient Tomb / 72
Glasnevin Cemetary Revisited / 73

VII
Afterimages / 75
Death of a Poet / 76
Snapshots of Jewish Amsterdam
  1. The Wibautstraat / 78
  2. The poetry and pathos of Social Democratic
     architecture / 79
  3. The Diamond Workers / 80
  4. Max Beckmann in Amsterdam, Winter 1944/1945 / 81
  5. Near the Portuguese Synagogue, Winter 1990/1991 / 82

VIII
Dublin 1982 / 83
Dublin 1987/The Salmon / 85
A Love Song in Ireland 1988 / 86
Dublin 1990/Emigration / 87
Ut Pictura Poesis / 88
The Words / 91
An Emigrant Ballad / 92

IX
Displacements
  1. The Old Fort in Leiden / 95
  2. Lost in Space / 96
  3. Homage / 97
Wolfe Tone / 98
Umlaut / 99
The Irony Of America / 100

X
To a Child in the Womb / 103
Birth Certificate: Amsterdam, 22 June 1988 / 104
Iceland / 105

1

THE CITY
after Cavafy

You say you will leave this place
And take yourself off to God-knows-where
A Galway cottage, a village in Greece
– Anywhere but here:
Paris, Alexandria, Finglas,
The grey eroding suburb
Where you squandered the coin of your youth.
You wander down to the carriageway
And watch the lorries speeding by.
Swooning in their slipstreams
You raise your eyes in a tropical dream
To the aeroplanes overhead.

But too late you realize
That you shall never leave here!
This, or next, or any other year.
You shall pass your life, grow old
In the same suburban lounge bars
Draining the dregs of local beers
Fingering a coin in your otherwise empty pockets.
And no matter how you toss it
It always turns up the same:
The plastic sun of Finglas
Squatting on every horizon.
The squandered coin of your youth!
The slot machines you fed have rung up blanks
Not just here, but everywhere.

YELLOW

I stamped through the pastures
booting the heads off buttercups
I stormed in out of the wheatfield
into a country kitchen
and let out my gurrier roar:
"Yellah! Yellah! Yellah!"
But she took me on her knee
and said: no, it's yellow
but that was a colour
I had never seen
till I saw her stretched on a hospital bed
the yellow of cancer and nicotine

MANDELSTAM

A woman's voice full of fear and pain
Dragged me awake
From my sleep's dark honey,
Blinking in the dark apartment
Like a flaccid wasp
Or something from Kafka.
I lay without moving.
And then the rattle and bark
Of her steel-tongued interrogator.
Plausible terror,
Uniformed chaos.
I got up and opened the door
And looked down the flood-lit corridor;
A man and a woman stood there
Talking and laughing
Like natural lovers.
They never even glanced at me.
I went back inside
Lay down on my bed
Tried to sleep but couldn't
With a needle stuck in my heart:
I heard what I heard
I heard what I heard

THE JOURNEY

for days the hum of rubber and oil
the screaming whisper of trucks
as they passed; we followed
a grey rainbow through
faceless green countryside;
kicked our heels in parking lots
a sentimental distance
from the road; drank coffee
in motorway stations clean
and familiar as a Hamburg whore.
2 a.m., 7 Klm. from the blue sign
for a cathedral town
slumbering in red brick.
we watched a flickering TV set
with the sound switched off
behind us we heard the ignition click
of spoon in coffee cup;
two men, commercial travellers we thought;
they followed us out to where
the road was picking up speed;
we drove off calm, wondering
down a stairway into the dark
while the night filled with static
and a song in another language
we sat flattened to our seats
while the night broke its limits
and the rectangle of our headlamps
became a square, and then
for a fraction of a second
a white line shooting
into the dead star
at the heart of things

CUCHULAINN

If I lived in this place for a thousand years
I could never construe you, Cuchulainn.
Your name is a fossil, a petrified tree
Your name means less than nothing.
Less than Librium, or Burton's Biscuits
Or Phoenix Audio-Visual Systems –
I have never heard it whispered
By the wind in the telegraph wires
Or seen it scrawled on the wall
At the back of the children's playground.
Your name means less than nothing
To the housewife adrift in the Shopping Centre
At eleven-fifteen on a Tuesday morning
With the wind blowing fragments of concrete
Into eyes already battered and bruised
By four tightening walls
In a flat in a tower-block
Named after an Irish Patriot
Who died with your name on his lips.

But watching TV the other night
I began to construe you, Cuchulainn;
You came on like some corny revenant
In a black-and-white made for TV
American Sci-Fi serial.
An obvious Martian in human disguise
You stomped about in big boots
With a face perpetually puzzled and strained
And your deep voice booms full of capital letters:
What Is This Thing You Earthlings Speak Of

BABEL

She is a language I will never speak
– great is my sorrow this night.
I will never whiten a wall for her
nor make the grass grow greener.
Her skin was the colour of honey
stored by the bees in the damp river bank
– where the sun himself had not kissed her
it was cream in a cool stone kitchen
in the stillness of a summer's day.

In the purple dusk by the walled-in river
she glowed as she stood in the street
I had never seen such a sight before
and even the traffic parted that she might pass.
Great was the sorrow I could not speak
in the room where we sat that night
– as a man who stands upon a hill
in a place of ancient renown
and hears a phrase of a song
float up from the valley below
like a wisp of white smoke
from a sacred fire
that burns in the sun at noon
– and he knows not what it speaks of
nor learning nor lonesome quest
through dusty book and library
shall be of any use to him.
Blessed is he who is her song!
Blessed with her skin of honey and cream
her perfect instep of soft kid's leather
and thigh like a pillar wrought
by some miraculous Greek.

Blessed is he, and cursed am I
with nothing to keep me from madness and death
but this dull unlovely translation!

COPENHAGEN DREAMING OF LENINGRAD

Warszava, the plaintive flute of the East,
Its ancient wooden melody bent
To the cello and drums of Moscow.

Over the drunken green Baltic
A black wind full of snow
Carries the straining orchestra.

Like the sand shifting beneath the waves,
Like the slash of flesh on bone!
Warszava, Warszava, I am drunk with your name

Till the glass-green Baltic floods
like the mind of a mad composer
With the wind's unplayable melody

And the mountains scale the ground
To a symphony's frozen climax!
The note is held and then begins

The slow bass beat of Stadt and Grad
– A shimmer, and water is frozen:
Seductive and brutal as massed violins
The choral cathedral of Lenin!

HAMLET IN DUBLIN

The trains have stopped running
The theatres are closed
My shoulders are bruised
From the narrow corridors
That lead out onto the stage

I rehearse all night in the bars
I stagger and fall, declaiming
And Oh my friends
There is something rotten
In this State of ours

The carpark echoes with my voice
The streetlamps blaze like footlights
And out in the darkness beyond them
I suddenly realise
There's no audience

BOXER

The days lurch towards me like a punch-drunk boxer
Swinging away with their horrible hammy fists
Pummelling away, unable to hurt me
– But I can't bring myself to avoid them,
With their battered Ernest Borgnine faces
And their cauliflower ears
And their stupid swollen horse's eyes
Begging me to let them win.

I can't bring myself to look at you
My head squats down on my chest
Like an old bag full of sawdust
And we continue, and the heart endures,
The heart in its red tent
A crushed head with a boxer's face
Its eyes clogged with blood
Blood streaming out of its ears

THE FUGITIVE

In the hour before the Metro opens
I remember you, Richard Kimble
With my hands dug deep in my jacket pockets
Walking the streets of a foreign city.

Tonight I suddenly remember it all –
The damp winter nights in Dublin
The living room with the curtain undrawn
And the streetlight spilling in

And myself, silent, hypnotised
Stretched out on the orange lino
Lost in the numinous images
Of the TV's black and white glow

And scarred by smoke and city dawns,
The muffled snarl of American accents
Coming in loud and razor sharp
Over the local interference.

I can't remember the stories now
But in the end it's only the ikons that matter,
The silent, anonymous, American city
With the rain running down the gutter

And the snatched glimpse of the one-armed man
Sinking back into the shadows,
The real victim, the truly guilty,
The man you're destined to follow.

This life, this city fits me
Like an old leather jacket
Picked up for nothing
In a second-hand market.

And I light up a cigarette
Relaxing in the casual rhyme
That floats through the city
Binding other lives to mine

And like so many times before
I turn up my collar against the wind
And walk off down the dark side of the street
Dreaming already of another town

Remembering you, Richard Kimble
And the way you taught me to live;
Ending another forgotten episode
Still myself, still the Fugitive.

TWO WOMEN

Nadezhda Mandelstam

In the damp brown evening of early winter
I see him stumbling along through the frozen mud
Across the bridge at the edge of town
With nothing but the broken harp of himself
On the forced march of days
Towards a battle he'd rather avoid
With his life, his hope,
Trudging a long way behind him
His music held tight in her aching fingers.

Lotte Lenya

Give her a tune and she'll break it they said
And she did, just like the world that she lived in.
The boys in the leather jackets
Were hardly surprised to find her
The goddess with the nightclub sneer
And a voice like the ruins of Berlin
Because no matter what they played on the radio
Day followed day like notes
In harsh, unheard-of harmonies
Where the tune can only survive
On the black bread of love.

II

AN IRISH REQUIEM
i.m. Mary Lynch (1897 - 1983)

Born in another country, under a different flag
She did not die before her time
Her god never ceased to speak to her.
And so she did not die. The only death that is real
Is when words change their meaning
And that is a death she never knew
Born in another country, under a different flag
When the soldiers and armoured cars
Spilled out of the ballads and onto the screen
Filling the tiny streets, she cried
And wiped her eyes on her apron, mumbling something
About the Troubles. That was a word
I had learned in my history book.
What did I care for the wails of the balding Orpheus
As he watched Eurydice burn in hell?
I was eleven years old,
And my Taoiseach wrote to me,
Born in another country, under a different flag.
She did not die before her time
She went without fuss, into the grave
She had bought and tended herself, with
The priest to say rites at her entry
And the whole family gathered,
Black suits and whiskey, a cortege
Of Ford Avengers inching up the cemetery hill.
Death came as an expected visitor,
A policeman, or rate collector, or the tinker
Who called every spring for fresh eggs,
Announced by the season, or knocks on walls,
Bats flying in and out of rooms, to signify
She did not die before her time
Her god never ceased to speak to her.

Till the last, he murmured in her kitchen
As she knelt at the chair beside the range
Or moved to the damp, unused, parlour
For the priest's annual visit.
Poete de sept ans, I sat on the polished wood,
Bored by the priest's vernacular harangue
As she knelt beside me on the stone church floor,
And overheard her passionate whisper,
Oblivious, telling her beads, and I knew
That I would remember this, that
Her god never ceased to speak to her.
As so she did not die. The only death that is real
Is when words change their meaning
And that is a death she never knew.
As governments rose and fell, she never doubted
The name of the land she stood on. Nothing
But work and weather darkened the spring days
When she herded her fattened cattle
Onto the waiting cars. It is not she who haunts
But I, milking her life for historical ironies,
Knowing that more than time divides us.
But still her life burns on, like the light
From a distant, extinguished star, and
O let me die before that light goes out
Born in another country, under a different flag!

III

THE SHARDS

"In the North we are not only on the cold edge of civilisation, but also on that of being, truth and life itself. Naked imaginative field..."
— Asger Jorn

1. The Bunkers

Along the great coast south of Bordeaux
The bunkers still stare out to sea
High-water marks of the black wave
That swept up out of the sump of Europe.
Untouched, they stand, undying monuments,
Easter Island heads in cold concrete.
On the side of one I found
Some Gothic lettering, black paint
That hadn't faded in the years of sun and wind.
But the blonde naked daughters
Sleep rough in them during the summer nights
And in the morning run laughing
Into the ocean their fathers had scanned.

2. The Birds

Somewhere north of Lille
I stared at the sea of white crosses,
Like sea birds resting on the earth.
So much suddenly real!

3. Frank Ryan Dead in Dresden!

The idea armed, like Ernie O'Malley
Another emerald-green incorruptible
Of course there was no place for the likes of you!
When you came bounding out of the prison camps
To join the shuffling battalions
Into the civil service offices
They gave you a job writing tourist brochures.
"Killarney is famous the wide world over
for the magnificent splendour
of its mountains and lakes . . ."
And after, you marched off into the night
To practise the illegal alchemy
Of slogans and heavy printer's ink.
Now it speeds up. A handsome head, in uniform.
Then defeat. The tale grows complex.
Europe dividing under your feet.
Conspiracies, betrayals, and all the rest.
In that last passport photo taken in Berlin
You look like Rembrandt in his last self-portrait.
There is much there I don't know, nor want to.
You followed your river into the sea,
And drowned, while your funeral pyre
Lit up the skies for a hundred miles around.

4. From a Diary

I seem to have travelled this landscape for years.
Brown hulks of deserted factories, the dark wounds
Of their shattered windows, fragments of glass
Defying the wind. The yellow blocks of flats
And behind them, the endless ordered fields
Flecked with rusted iron.
The train slowed down near a flat broad river
And I saw fields full of green machines
Stretching out into the distance,
Tensing on black rubber. A lone sentry
Stood out against the skyline, looking in no
Particular direction. Behind him a filthy grey sky
Floundered into the night.

5. Heinrich Böll in Ireland

We slept through it. A stray bomber,
A black sheep strayed from the pack
Came crackling in out of the watching darkness.
Later, some stumbled across our shores
In search of a green poultice
For wounds we couldn't have understood.
There, at last, a small destiny, ours.
This also; the skyways criss-crossed
By peaceful jets, their passengers reading
In magazines about the
Most profitable
Industrial
Location
In Europe.

6. Concert-Going in Vienna

Our houses are open tombs that will survive us.
As so are our lives. No one survives a war like that.
That is obvious; also ridiculous.
Our eyes blink in the sullen gleam of the knife
But do not see the submerged balancing weight
Beneath the cutting edge. Tonight, I feel it
The solid drag, the tug and undertow
Of centuries of prosperity, watching
These faces and manners planed by music,
I had not thought death had missed so many.
This woman here in front of me, for instance
In pearls and grey hair in a stately bun
Nodding her head in time to Bruckner's Fourth.
She is not dead, nor am I. The sublime
And gracious she samples as familiar delicacies
And it is churlish of me to criticise this.
But still, I know, from the ranks of satisfied diners
A hungry ghost slips off into the forest
Trying on coats of clay for size.

7. The Boys of '69

"I don't know why we didn't go –
we talked about nothing else."
But they didn't go, didn't die
On the barricades of '69,
They survived to cushy jobs
In Luxembourg and Brussels.
Cushy but hopeless!
"Sure we hadn't a chance boy!
What do you think?
The French and the Dutch
were already dug in."
He peels the silver wrapping
Off another bottle of beer.
I watch the alien sun sink red
Behind the blocks of flats.
"Poor Sean! They found his body
out there on the beach. Nothing
ever proved, of course. Never
saw him depressed. A boy
to drink though! He was barred
from the British Embassy
after that night,
I remember it well . . ."
I suddenly see him, poor Sean,
With his Aran sweater
And second-class degree in history
A pale-faced corpse
Drifting like a dead fish
Through a sea of foreign newsprint
Red-bearded idol of a scattered army
Of terylene shirts and expense accounts
In half the capital cities of Europe . . .

8. The Shards

For months, coming home late at night
We would stop at a traffic light
In the middle of nowhere
And sit there, the engine restless
For the empty motorway
While I looked out at the half-built flyover
That stood in the moonlight
Like a ruined Greek temple
And I suddenly felt surrounded
By the shattered and potent monuments
Of a civilisation we have not yet discovered
The ghost of something stalking us
The future imagined past perhaps
Or else the millions of dead
Rising and falling
Into the mud and carved stone
The ghost of the beast
Whose carapace we inhabit
Not knowing if we stand
At centre or circumference
Sensing that shards are our only wholeness
Carefully carving their shattered edges.

IV

IN THE SUBURBS

". . . the whole world is suburb
Where are the real towns?"
— Marina Tsetaeva.

1. A Letter To Marina Tsetaeva

In white rooms looking out on the city
I woke up alone with you, Marina Tsetaeva.
Her body is a sheet of cold white flame
Where I am burned to translucence;
In her hair I smelt Prague and damnation
And music tearing through flesh
Like the pull of a planet.
Her mocking schoolgirl's laugh
Her arched dancer's calf
Her feet in white boots like elegant hooves!

Who else
Could I pray
To watch over her
In the darkness where she moves.

2. The Music Lesson

In white rooms looking out on the city
Filled with light like flat champagne
We woke to that aboriginal heat
And walked out into the warm rain.

It sprinkled its dusty benediction
On the Sunday morning pavements
Streaked the windows of our train
Through the passionate clay of the mountains.

When we reached the town I left you behind
Walked out into the almond trees
And sat in the dust in the dead afternoon
Surrounded by my own emptiness

Watching the distant mountain range
Whose name I couldn't remember
Feeling everything drop away
Into the static sweating air.

With the year dying all around me, I walked
Back to the house where I'd left you singing
Like a man approaching his execution
For a cause he no longer believed in.

I turned away into the future
And watched you go
Like a man stepping through
A plate-glass window.

3. In the Suburbs

Closing my eyes I sink down into a darkness
Where your absence is the only presence.
Open again to a shout of light
Two lip-sticked girls, a glass of beer
Push you back into fragile limits.
I leave the bar and move out
Into the raw streets of this half-built suburb
Stepping over virgin pavements
And violated earth
Through a mesh of lives just beginning
And I'm the only prisoner
Of this heavy spring evening, this dull suburb
Unable to mortgage my life to the future.

4. The Knot

When a note is played
The pause that follows
Is no longer silence.

FROM A CAFÉ

*"Fósforo y fósforo en la oscurided,
lagrima y lagrima en la polvareda."*
– César Vellego

Last night I dreamt you were in my room.
In my sleep I felt your presence
Like fine rain on my nerve ends
But when I struggled awake you were gone.

You've blown through me like nuclear fallout
And left me reeling, sick in my bones
Nursing my sickness in suburban cafés
Where the coffee bubbles with faith in mankind.

Match after match in the dark
Tear after tear in the dust
The waitress brings me cup after cup
While I hide my face in a foreign tongue.

ON BOARD

I see you asleep in our old room
The soft shine of your hands
And eyelids, like a fish's belly
In a dark ocean.

Outside, lit up
And throbbing with emptiness
The city pads through the night
Like a great space station.

The waves
Of your sleeping body
Rise and fall
On my mind's ragged edge.

Hours ago,
I peeled away from your side
Hurtled off
Into outer darkness

But left my poetry
To watch over your bed
A black angel
Caught in the mesh of your hair.

IN A BATHROOM

Venus emerging from a porcelain shell
You step out of the bath, and stand there, dripping
With a towel wrapped tight about your head
Your face deathly white in a beauty mask.

A carnal nun, angst in high heels.
You always look the way I feel
With your mouth twisted by music
Your nails stained with the blood of lies!

I sit here watching you move about
Thinking of how I love you
But can think of nothing but Lorca
And the smell of the sun on my leather jacket.

THE CHORD

We stand in an ocean
Of melted light. It is dusk.
The smell of eucalyptus
On the chilled city air
The glow of streetlights
Behind the dark leaves.
You bow your head before me
Under a pain I can't understand.
That I have caused it
I sense dimly, like an animal
Or a man looking at a painting
By some old master,
Full of forgotten allegory.
I am silent,
Appalled at my own existence
Unable to move an inch
Away from you,
or nearer.

POSTHUMOUS

Something is pushing against my blood.
From the bus I watch the children
Set fire to sheets of paper
And scatter them, screaming, into the wind.
They burn down to nothing,
A black smudge on the concrete
Bleeding its greyness into the sky.
I think of Siberia, how clean it is.
I move around the city, denounced
To the secret police of popular songs.
A name flares in the darkness.
Moon-sister, twin.
Who are you? I don't know.
My mouth tastes of splintered bone.
I thought I'd left this place a long time ago.

V

"La source est roc et la langue est tranchée"
— René Char

THE DIARY OF A SILENCE

In Parnell Square it's always raining
On the junk heap of history where I was born
One wet night, in the Rotunda Hospital
While the crowds surged down O'Connell Street
And the shades did cluster round
My state-assisted birth, in this elephant's
Graveyard under grey skies!

The damp, disintegrating houses
Shuffle shoulder to shoulder through time
Stuffed with religious statues and creaking
Rooms, empty, forgotten, memorial halls
Marked by cracked plaques and faded signs
Of chipped gilt over fanlights
Everything living its posthumous existence
Hungering in me for an image
That is not mere archaeology
The casual coupling of history and self.

I probed the city's cracked grey ribs,
Noted the casual irony
Of the tottering Georgian tenements!
But one day they were gone
Thesis devoured by antithesis
Oratory swallowed by irony
Cancelling each other out
Leaving not even an aftertaste
Just silence tensing towards the word
That will define it,
In a language that doesn't yet exist.

Where the buildings once had stood
The sky rushed into their virgin spaces
The mad light of Dublin battering my face
The great expressionist winter sky

Where light and dark wrestle like primitive gods
Like complex chemical formulae
Something struggling to become itself:

It has always been like this. What can be said
Is not worth saying, will not still the itch
That has always possessed me, gripped
And held fast from the start
And would not release, or burst into flower
Except suddenly, laboriously,
Like turning the corner into Parnell Square
To see the yellow buses throbbing in the rain
Pristine, orphic; obmutescent.

TWO POEMS FOR PADDY GRAHAM

1. *Summer in Monaghan*

my mouth is daubed with black and green!
gulping mouthfuls of dark air
black flags hang from the telegraph poles
this land is a hunger
I cannot breathe
love lies like a plague on the land
love? the greyness of summer?
(who are those faces, bright
and I think, familiar,
names, old loves, stirring
like nails in their rusty sockets)

a black sea rocks us to sleep

in the morning the darkness lightens
between the murderous drumlins
the roads are smeared
with small furred corpses
sometimes a sweet rain rinses the air
water colours a faint illusion
(in the dead hiss of a summer's evening
a lake has drifted from Persia)

2. *Heimat*

All over Ireland the black light falls.
On the rotting stone houses of
Provincial towns,
And on the pristine office blocks;
On the nervous green fields
And cold suburban roads.
This was home, as a child I knew it.
The black clouds soaked in radiance
Exploding softly on the Wicklow Mountains
Marching west in a dinosaur train
Across the wet slate roofs, bobbing
Heavily forward with brute momentum
And grace, leaving their footprints
In my mind, deserts hungry
For remembered weather,
Like your canvas hungry for paint
Each painting a difficult homecoming
A muddy thaw, savage archaeology, the slow
Decolonisation of childhood,
Letting us see
What is in the black light visible.

THREE FRAGMENTS ON THE THEME OF MOVING AROUND IN CITIES

I. Epitaph for Matt Talbot

"Skua!" "Skua!", the gulls shriek
Skiting above the stinking Liffey
Where your name flaps
Like a plastic sack
Along the deserted quays
In the minds of old women
Carrying their shopping
From chapel to chapel.

II. Little Suburban Ode

In our cold, gloomy Napoli
Pasolini's Nordic children
Cruise the icy pot-holed streets
In stolen diplomatic limos

Rocketing round the broken corners
Like steel balls in a pinball game
Before they fly right off the board
– Or slot home safely in the suburbs.

III. Berlin

Under a bruised sky the empires meet
And freeze. I don't like that I like it here,
The cold stench of flesh become stone
The palled appalling innocence of the heart
A giddy dog loping through ruins
A god on the morning of creation
His mouth full of juicy bones.

ONE VERSION OF A MYTH

I scribbled poems
in the back of
my chemistry notebook
about the survival
of primitive man
into the techno-
logical era.
But they didn't
answer my question.
At evening I always
found myself here
in one place or another
watching the dusk descend
on the shuttered suburbs
splash the skyline
with the chemical red
and then
the light was gone –
suddenly swallowed
by billowing clouds
of octopus black –
tomorrow it would return
in lines
of field-grey infantry
straggling in
across the coast road
and the frozen sand
choked on the corpses
of birds
and old rubber tyres.

I stood
on this cold battlefield
choking on fear
and the February air

walked
between the silent blocks
the steel-grilled shops
the streets shuttling
endlessly
back into each other –
I felt that we were
strapped tight
hurtling towards
some moment in space and time
we could not construe
or else that this speed
was the illusion of stasis
there was no escape
no meaning
in this prison
of concrete and night
– I lit cigarettes
and smoked them
to communicate
with some heroic spirit
remembered from my childhood
– I consoled myself
with the sound
of my steel-heeled boots
on the plates
of the railway bridge

SEA FISHING

We knelt on the back-door steps
Banging sparks out of cement
With heavy hammers and strips of lead
Which we bent and folded in clumsy lumps
And boiled in a blackened pan
Huddled round like alchemist's apprentices
To watch its shabby dull grey surface
Wrinkle and soften and shine forth
Suddenly into miraculous molten silver
Which hissed and globbed in the holes
We moulded in tins of wet sand
To harden and dull once more, but now
Transformed, shaped to our purpose;
The day when we'd make our way
To the water's edge, to lean against
The wind and cast our weights out far
Into the inscrutable sea, to wait
For the answering tug,
Men with a raison d'etre;
To coax from the ocean's leaden bass
A single, gleaming, note
A silver-scaled bass.

INTENSITY, EXALTATION
after Vallejo

I want to write, but I foam at the mouth
There's so much to say but I get bogged down;
There's no number uttered which isn't a sum,
No pyramid written without a green heart.

I want to write, but I sense the puma;
I ask for laurel, but they give me an onion.
There's no sound made which doesn't grow vague,
There's neither god nor son of god without development.

So come on then, let's eat grass,
Fruit of weeping, flesh of moans,
Jam made out of our melancholy souls.

Come on! Come on! I am wounded;
Let's drink what's already been turned into piss,
Come on, mister crow, let's go to your missus.

ELEGY FOR THE UNKNOWN SOLDIER

"It is hard to read on the ancient stone . . .
In the month of Athyr Levkios fell asleep."
                                        – Cavafy

One evening in August, the light already failing
An insurance salesman dropped me off at a crossroads
In Cavan or Monaghan, the beginning of the drumlin
                                                country
I stood there for a while, near a newly-built bungalow
Watching the green fields darken behind a screen of
                                                hedges.
Just where the roads met there was a sort of green
With a JCB parked right up on the verge
And a small celtic cross of grey granite.
I walked over to read the inscription
Peering through the fading light.
"Patrick O'Neill, Volunteer, Third Belfast Brigade
Shot on a nearby hillside. 16 April 1923."
I can't remember exactly, but that was the gist of it.
By the time I finished reading, it was completely dark.
All the lights were on in the nearby bungalow,
I could see the TV screen through the living-room window.
I heard the engine of a car in the distance,
The cone of its headlights appearing and disappearing.
He stopped and gave me a lift to Cootehill. I didn't look
                                                back.

THE EAST WIND

Straight from Siberia, our mothers said,
The East wind blew in off the Irish Sea
To freeze us between the rows of houses
Where we ran in the glaring yellow light
To chase a dirty white plastic ball
Skittering along the concrete.

Our faces were frozen in monkey grins,
Our hands were completely numb
And when we fell flying onto the pavement
We did not feel a thing, nor stop
To check our limbs, but struggled up
To woodenly run on, not thinking
Of the relief and pain that would come
With the thaw.

THE BLACK PIANO

The language turns to mush in our mouths –
Like the brown slush flooding the streets
Beneath my window. But now it's snowing,
White flakes falling on the frozen canals.
In my room, I turn the pages of Russian books
Trying to understand, knowing
That the storm that swept them away
Is the storm that swept me here
To stand in the place where they once stood
My head ringing with their echoes.
Through the wall of my room I hear
The tuneless tentative notes
Of my neighbour's pupils,
Their fingers stumbling over the keyboard.
Coming home late at night, I like
To climb the steps and peer
Into her tiny front room,
Filled with a frozen black piano
Basted with hidden light, like a shrine.
In my room I stalk on,
Imagining listeners behind the white wall
Their ears bent to the tuneless tentative sound
Of my black boots plodding through virgin snow.

VALPARAISO

He sat in the gloom like a dim buddha
His bald oval head gleaming
In the faint light filtering into the room.
There was a smell of damp earth in the hallway
The heavy long sadness of ancient forest floors
Where the sun has never shone. We entered
From the chilly marble stairs, still splashed
With light and shouts from the street outside
And stumbled over the screens and tapestries
Low sofas festooned with Indian designs
That he patiently crafted here, in the back streets
Of a tourist town.
                  He was no Indian, though silent
And patient as one, and his large brown eyes
Were like the stolen eggs of some exotic bird
That dreams of mountains and circling, circling
Through brilliant skies. The light
Assaulted the blinds that hadn't been open in years
Filtering into the room in slits
Illuming snatches of dust.
Someone whispered his story in my ear, the usual
One I'd heard before; economist
In the Allende government, flight and exile,
His wife had left him for a minor diplomat,
Leaving him with children behind.
But none of this seemed relevant to his immobile
Vegetable sadness, which raddled the air
Like a dry stain. His son put on his leather jacket
Went out to hunt *rubias* in the local discos
Up on the roof I bounced a ball
With his neurotic daughter
Her vowels already rounded by Catalan.
Later that night, Luis arrived to cook the meat.
Nervy garrulous, Argentinian,
Cursing Spain and leaving it behind him,

His tickets home already bought.
We talked about Borges and Spanish football
Our faces red with the heat of the coals
While down in the streets, the tourists drifted
Through valleys of floodlit sculptured flowers.
I woke next morning before anyone else,
And padded through the hallway. Through the open door
I saw him laid on his bed like a toppled idol,
Barely breathing, in the other bed his daughter
Restless and creased, a dark snake in the undergrowth.
The light drilled into the walls. Outside,
It was Sunday on the beach, the trains
Came lurching and rocking out of Barcelona
Searing in the heat, packed with people
Their limbs already turning brown.
Before we left that afternoon
We sat once more in the gloom to sing some songs
And he strummed a simple melancholy dance
Over and over again, on the strung shell of a armadillo,
And falling through the years,
I saw a winter's morning of fear and booming voices
My hands cold clutching the varnished wood
While I painfully glossed a Gaelic poem
About a ship sailing out of Valparaiso
And how its purple echo had sailed with me
To this strange harbour, this unmappped land,
To dance now to the Charrango!

ANNE FRANK

What we cannot speak about,
we must pass over in silence . . .

Life is lived in rooms like this.
That, at least, we can say.
And people come and go
On speakable missions,
Clear commands. And we can talk
And smother the air with words
Till we feel we understand.

In these rooms we sleep and dream,
And rise to breakfast on white linen.
There are books to read,
And at night the scratch
Of pen and paper.

Life is lived in rooms like this
Where we lean towards a square of light
But where the walls are
We can only discover
By walking out into that darkness
Fingers outstretched, blind
Knowing we have no words
For what we may find.

EXILES

In all the dead ends of Dublin
you will find the Italian chippers
abandoned, forgotten consulates
of obscure Apennine villages
whose chocolate-box picture
sometimes hangs
above the bubbling frier.
Again and again,
they dispense our visas
sealed with salt and vinegar
wrapped in greaseproof paper.
Somehow we never go.

The old consul
has grown sardonic.
He stares out the steamed-up
windows at the rain,
the file of bored taximen
waiting at the rank.
His eyes glint with vendetta.
He lights up another Sweet Afton

turns to glare at his sons
who have mastered the local dialect,
leaning across the counter
to chat with their friends.
Sometimes, without warning
they all begin
to shout in Italian
like Joyce and his children.

ON HEARING MICHAEL HARTNETT READ HIS POETRY IN IRISH

First, the irretrievable arrow of the military road
Drawing a line across all that has gone before
it's language a handful of brutal monosyllables.

By the side of the road the buildings eased up;
The sturdy syntax of castle and barracks
The rococo flourish of a stately home

The formal perfection and grace
Of the temples of neoclassical government
The avenues describing an elegant period. Then,

The red-brick constructions of a common coin
To be minted in local stone, and beyond them
The fluent sprawl of the demotic suburbs

Tanged with the ice of its bitter nights
Where I dreamt in the shambles of imperial iambs,
Like rows of shattered Georgian houses.

I hear our history on my tongue,
The music of what has happened!
The shanties that huddled around the manor

The kips that cursed under Christchurch Cathedral
Rising like a madrigal into the Dublin sky
– But tonight, for the first time,

I heard the sound
Of the snow falling through moonlight
Onto the empty fields.

THE REAL THING

I shuffled the musty floorboards
Of your emporium, stuffed with baubles
And useless knick-knacks, melancholy
Mechanical toys from Hong Kong, that soon
Fell asunder, scattering pieces of coloured tin
And stone-age plastic all over the house,
Like indecipherable relics.

Where did you come from? I like
To think of you, a grey-bearded shuffler
Peddling your goods all round the Baltic
From Lübeck and Lublin to Dublin
Where the pale children from the nameless suburbs
Gawked at your gaudy mortal balloons
Their fingers and eyes hungry for gewgaws.

After the war, you imported thousands
Of plywood fiddles, and sold them
At half-a-crown apiece, to some old fiddler;
Who would take them and bury them in shallow
Graves, in the uncertain soil of Dublin gardens
For six months or more, to resurrect them
Like Viking bones, grown moldy and seasoned
Their ears clogged with gritty earth;
To sell them all summer long
At feises and fleadhs all over the country.
And no one could tell them from the real thing.

LATIN AS A FOREIGN LANGUAGE

I suppose I should feel somehow vindicated
   To see our declensions bite deeper
      Than our legionaries' swords –
         But somehow I don't.
      We're a mixed lot here, devils
   To drink; old senatorial types and
Discarded favourites, poets without patrons etc.

When asked why they're here they might answer
   About duty to the empire, missionary zeal
      Or simply the spirit of adventure –
         All rot, of course.
      No one leaves Rome unless
   He has to, or not exactly because he has to
Like a vulgar soldier in a conscripted legion.

But things somehow conspire to force him out.
   Not all poets find patrons, not all
      Fits smoothly into public life –
         You know how it is.
      One wrong word in the wrong ear.
   One fateful opportunity fluffed, and
You may as well forget it. Who understands these things?

Some say they lie in the lap of the gods but either way
   We end up here in the backwaters of empire
      Drumming our illustrious tongue
         Into barbarian skulls
      And polishing up the phrases
   Of the oafs who govern in Rome's name.
Like I said, a mixed lot, refugees all from obscure failures.

Some marry local girls, and sprout blonde beards
   And curls overnight. Poor bastards!

How can they take seriously
Those bovine bodies
Those gaudy faces lisping bad breath.
Who could write poetry for such as these?
I think about these things a lot, but come to no conclusion

During the freezing winter nights sitting round the wine
And olives, telling tales of sunnier days
Sucking ancient bits of gossip
Down to the dry pit
Cato elaborates his pet theory;
How Rome will someday crumble to dust
Beneath the barbarian heel, and only our precious language

Will survive, a frail silken line flung across the years
But I don't know. Who among these barbarians
Would give a fart in his bearskin
For Horace or Virgil
Or any of us? All they want is enough
To haggle with a Sicilian merchant, or cheat
The Roman tax collector out of his rightful due.

But late at night, when I stumble out into
The sleet and cold I was not born to
And feel the threatening hug
Of those massive forests
Stuffed with nameless beasts
And the great godless northern sky
Threatening me with its emptiness and indifference

To me and all that are like me – then, sometimes,
I think he may be right; that
We are the galley slaves
Sweating below
Bearing the beautiful
Princess who sits in the prow
Across the ocean to her unknown lover.

VI

GLASNEVIN CEMETERY

With deportment learnt from samurai films
I surface in the ancestral suburbs.
My grandmother is older than China,
Wiser than Confucius.
I pace my stride to hers
Soaking in the grey-green air.

Under my name cut in stone
My grandfather lies
Within hearing of the lorries' roar
Out on the main road.
I forget my unseemly haste
To see the Emperor's tomb.

We search for family graves
In the suburbs of the dead.
From the jumble of worn stones
Unmarked by celtic crosses
Like an egyptologist she elucidates
Obscure back-street dynasties.

We see where Parnell lies buried
Under Sisyphean stone
Put there my father says
To keep him from climbing out.
I am surprised by ancient bitterness
Surfacing among the TV programmes.

The plotters of the nation
Are niched in their kitsch necropolis.
Matt Talbot, Larkin, Michael Collins
A holy graven trio
Shoulder to shoulder enshrined
In the tidy bogomil parlour of her heart.

The day flowers sluggishly
From the stone of contradictions.
The trees sway like green hasidim
I shuffle in a kind of lethargic dance
A sprung sign among the signified
A tenant in the suburbs of silence.

CIGARETTE ELEGY

Nobody smokes like the men of my childhood
with their *Woodbines, Sweet Afton,*
Players's Navy Cut, flashing eternally white
and virginal in their stained hands
the dark gold of the tobacco gleaming
in the grime of the morning busses
trundling through the streets. How they inhaled
the metallic smoke, like two gauntlets
hard, black, reaching down into their lungs
to grip like a hammer the heart's worn handle!
They inhaled, with gulps, like men
drinking the wine that had been promised
as if each one was a disaster averted
a moment won back from the devourer of time
their eyes focused on no point
their sunken cheeks sucked in silence
like a hummingbird swallowing sweetness.
But you, you never exhaled,
no, you held your breath, singing dumb
till your unwritten skin turned yellow
and cracked, and what does it matter
if they inhaled you deep
in the earth's brown lung
or consumed you as you once consumed
in the fire that watches men, cigarettes
and stars go out one by one
to be not reborn?

THE SONG OF THE EARTH:
EPITAPH FOR A DUBLINER OF THE FIFTIES

Right from the start you were underground
Never sticking your head above the parapet.
Passive resistance, acceptance, survival,
Call it what you like. Your weapons:
Evasion, drink, conformity, laughter. I hesitate
To use the obvious Ostblok/Diaspora metaphors
But they fit. Listening to the babble on the streets
I try to translate you into a grey, truthful voice
But it's not yours. When I write your life's Yiddish
It reads like bad German:
We swallowed our Hebrew a long time ago.

Now you've crossed the river to the third shore.
In the grave you'll speak with a mouth full of earth
You'll stay silent and let them smell the rot of your breath.

NIGHT IN THE SUBURBS OF DUBLIN

Kept awake by conscience
And nineteenth century coughs
I try to crash the language barrier,
Soliloquising for hidden cameras.
Someone groans, an everyday ache
Not worth talking about.
I listen, I breathe.
Language is a listening-glass
A lung breathing the earth.
Useless . . . the susurrating darkness
Ulcerates: a dog howls
Like a god remembering the world
He meant to create
But couldn't find the words for.

A PROTESTANT GRAVEYARD IN COUNTY MONAGHAN

The stone of the church is warm to the touch,
mottled by sodden zephyrs.
The grass lisps a mute stone anthem:
we lay down on the earth
and wrapped its damp plaid round us.

Inflamed by autumn,
a tree blazes silently
like the flag of the perfect country.

AT THE GRAVE OF FATHER HOPKINS

Outlandish accent in ancestral earth!
The clods drift and turn
through your sightless skies.
You are here, reluctant guest
at the wedding feast of Dublin's dead.

In this hated here, you shed
your unloved body to be married
in the earth with the humble
whose words you plundered
for the still storms of your poems.

Underground, who knows,
they seeped out of your crumbling ears
to rhyme with memories of
Christmas trees on O'Connell Street
and the hidden starlings' tinsel blaze.

Often I bore them, your poems,
past your unsprung presence
but they never called to you
nor you to them. No wonder:
you had gone one remove further

to achieve your final version.

WORDS ON AN ANCIENT TOMB

Resist! Think how the carved stone
dams your life,
think how tradition begins
with your next word
and be deaf to the vulgar rant
of the authorized ghost.

Do not resist the day
which turns to stone in your mouth.
You are a bull
who has learned to eat air.
Listen! – how your heart verbs
the waiting dust.

GLASNEVIN CEMETERY REVISITED

The ghosts of machines danced
excruciatingly in their bones.
Coins chipped their hands.

Their bodies lie in the earth
like wet fires, discarded shards
in the potter's field.

Groundlings
in the shadow of words
secreting silence.

The trees *whisht:*
silence veils the rant.
The day sinks to hush.

Flesh is their marble in mortmain.
They left me a fee hand
to tremble above their palimpsest.

And yet their blessing wounds;
their pain infects this page:
our alphabets are maculate.

VII

AFTERIMAGES

I looked out the kitchen window
down into the street
and the eyes
of a neighbour woman
being carried on a stretcher
into her house to die.

The women were hoisting you
onto the couch
when our eyes met:
that this could happen
to any mother's son!
That even Groucho Marx
was a member of this club!

Eve's belly
was smooth as a wheatfield,
rope of nothingness
snaking through the eyes.

That night, we played
all the Requiems we had:
Verdi, Brahms, Mozart . . .
at each record's centre
the navel of death.

I thought of the black whore
I saw in Amsterdam
framed in her allegorical window
shining like polished darkness,
how her Day-Glo purple girdle
gorged the light.

DEATH OF A POET

"Der Tod ist ein Meister aus Deutschland"
— Paul Celan

Why did I find it so hard to talk to you?
It wasn't just your deafness, or my own
smirking guilt at being at home in this age.
No, it was something more. We disagreed
on nothing of importance, but I hated your life
hated your house arrest in your own survival.
I didn't want to believe your life could happen
because it offered no room for redress
— and I was too Irish to go that naked.
Often, you mentioned the Mayor of Cork,
how as a youth in Haarlem you followed
his hunger strike, his slow descent into victory.
McSw-*ee*-ney or McSw-*eye*-ney, you always asked
with the attentiveness of the autodidact.
But of course I never knew. On dark mornings,
descending the stairs in the coffin-narrow house,
I would hear your brisk shuffle in the study
already haunting your own books, and I thought:
it has always been like this. Just once,
at a party, you angular with alcohol
spouting Hölderlin to some German girl,
I glimpsed you as you must have been —
blond, bony adolescent in love with that
language's deadly mirror, those black waves
soon to break in your ears, and your diamond boss's
comic despair, sending you out
to write poems in the café at the corner.
After, you built a house in the dunes
and kept your eyes fixed on the sea
your ears pinned like butterflies.
That curious stance of yours . . .
shoulders bent, head raised expectant.

Even then, in those '50s' photos with your daughters
I see how you were pointed elsewhere. Even then,
you were waiting, with what patience,
with what longing, you were waiting
for the angel to return and kiss your heart to ash.

SNAPSHOTS FROM JEWISH AMSTERDAM

1. *The Wibautstraat*

It's years since this city froze.
The water is soft and stinking,
the tourist boats circle aimlessly.

In the evenings I emerge
from the city's watery maze
like a weevil from a cheese

to stand here near your monument:
a four-lane highway
out to the suburbs

where I too could have been born
in the resurrected '50s
to hopeful parents

in public parks
holding us up like offerings
to shiny new Kodaks

and in the evenings,
kicked a ball with Johan Cryff
down endless concrete summers.

Now I loiter and listen
for the whirr of angel wings
the screech of diamond on diamond.

Nightly, grey water sluices
through my veins while I wait for
the first brittle grin of ice.

2. *The poetry and pathos of Social Democratic architecture*

The trick is to make red brick
perform like natural stone, to build
the diamond city that lives in the blood,
that wants to crystallize
in words and acts
but so often settles back
smouldering, like lumps
of half-burnt coal on the landscape.
Fuck Hegel. This is different.
This is the diamond we are born with
or better, the diamond we are
no matter how softly accoutered
the head gnawing itself
in hunger, like a hard flame.

3. The Diamond Workers

An obvious one. Saved,
like the best wine, only till last

they did what they had always done
until, on the day of the last razzia

they stood with their arms in the air
and let the diamonds trickle down

to form a pool of salted light
in which they stood, stranded

Later, a soldier gathered them up
with a sweeping brush.

4. *Max Beckmann in Amsterdam, Winter 1944/1945*

The road from one day to the next
crosses a narrow bridge
across the Amstel river,

takes him through the emptying streets
rehearsing the operas
of the future.

The winter is hungry for men
its swollen sky
and gluttonous light.

Like ambulant masscards,
the people he passes are ringed
with icy black auras.

At the zoo,
the hippo floats
in the foul water

like the world's sum total
of intransitive verbs.
His mind full of hippo,

Beckmann feasts his brush
on Quappi's thighs, and waits
for the squadrons of platitude
to arrive at the City Gates.

5. Near the Portuguese Synagogue, Winter 1990/1991

Hell has frozen over
and the children skate upon it,
their steel carves the ice
into a jewel of perfect absence.
So let the diamond fall from your hand,
leave it uncut,
a raw fragment of stone in the heart:
let the business-like dusk reveal
a box of left-behind light.

VIII

DUBLIN 1982

Broken and sad as dusk in an Asian city
an Orientalist landscape
crookedly hung on a concrete wall.

You have half-forgotten your lover's names.
You married a boor and built a hurdle
your children couldn't jump.

You will not recognise them
prefer to watch your decay in the mirror
a stranger to yourself

a displaced person from wars
fought on your streets, wandering
in the world's washed-up trash.

Your buildings collapse like Berlin
in slow motion: your wall is still intact
and sometimes visible.

Out of your dead meteorite heart
the suburbs are scattered like rubble
a no-man's-land between tenses

barbarians at the gates of Rome
hiding behind the names
of rustic villages.

Your children are all exiles
whether they stay or go:
in your mad microclimate

the heart swears allegiance to nothing
but the palm trees swaying
in freezing rain.

DUBLIN 1987 / THE SALMON

The salmon is what the river sings.
You swim in my blood like a dull crystal.

My blood silvers and deepens.
You grow in my brain like lichen.
You are my concussion.

You are the place
Where thirst is slaked with thirst.

A LOVE SONG IN IRELAND, 1988

I'll love you till the end of time
He said, a dark cave opening
At the edge of his words.

The round silver names
Were in his mouth,
The warm mud,

Their sleep is water.
They float together.
Each night his prayer is the same:

Let us dive, let us be propelled
By the thick engine
Of our love,

Let us be the salmon
Who follows a river
Through poisoned seas.

DUBLIN 1990/EMIGRATION

This country's half-life
is running out, and still they leave
leaving half-lives behind
to stretch their traces across the globe
to live the life that is left to them;
and to know this, always:
We ourselves alone have made the weather
And I myself alone could do no better.

UT PICTURA POESIS

Our fascinations draw us
– towards what?
Our selves, the truth, to be
repeated and repeated
biological acts?

Maybe they just draw us.
I only know that patrolling galleries
something in me is woken and soothed
by the savage poultice
of Beckmann and Munch

with the velvet crunch
of mirrors mating
a pen bursting
into silence
drowning out the scratch of letters.

But now, out of that blue
nick of ink
on the tongue
a word bubbles into my mouth:
Cumiskey!

Those displaced syllables . . .
My ear remembers his aura
orphaned among the O's and Macs
blue angel of memory
sharing my bench in drawing class
where I pose in my mind's eye
at the end of that first decade.
See my small black heart!
Sulky Marrano,
Making the sign of the cross.

My left hand hung useless
plotting the future
my right hand
aped the ways of men
drawing a landscape I'd never seen:

a white cottage with yellow roof,
stack of turf against the wall
and behind, the Marian skies
the brown pyramid
mountains –

the Free State ikon,
to be executed daily
till its imperfections
were caught to perfection
a prayer repeated till it cursed.

But Cumiskey was different.
Though scooped like us
from Irish muck,
the skies of another Europe
leaked through his hands

till everything he touched
turned the muddy blue
of reality: people, houses,
hills, horses, were all alike
were all like

some Black Theatre, some
shadowgraph smeared
with tears and hunger,
Plato's cave converted
to a bomb shelter.

I looked away from his paper
to the skies beyond the window
smudged, sinister
in that moment
before the lights come on.

They never do. The picture's jammed.
Starlings fall dead
from my nerve ends
and the drying paint
mourns the light.

THE WORDS

The rusted sword which wields me, say,
is skittering down the rocks of a Wicklow mountain
scattering into a film of light
leaving the scree.

Somewhere a sea gull shrieks
and lifts itself into the air,
heart's luftwaffe,
skirling leitmotiv

of my slow sixteenth summer
when I sat in my room reading *Ulysses*
looking out over the city
to the Sugerloaf mountain.

One dull Sunday I charged up its slopes
faoi geasa to reach the summit or die
the earth falling away beneath me
the ocean vaulting up behind

to find when I reached the summit
I had become a cardboard profile of myself.
O static weightless wrestling
to get the light behind me

and shoulder my shadow onto the page
to neither speak nor move
but lie here and not lie
like a dam across the river

and let the flow obliquely tell
the words whose meaning I am
through which I pass
like a slow bullet!

AN EMIGRANT BALLAD

The suburbs of Dublin
are full of roads
which lead to nowhere
breaking off abruptly
in mountains of churned-up mud.
Like unfinished sentences
they say: "I love – ",
"I hope for – ", "I dream of – ".
Once I thought that all
these roads led somewhere, some –
but it's better not to
give it a name.

This road leads to the airport.
In the departure lounge,
a young man approaches me,
a ticket in his large red hands.
He asks if I know the way
to the plane for London. I do.
"Do you mind if I follow you?" he asks.

And he does, a few yards behind.
Whenever I look over my shoulder,
at the top of the escalator
at the cash register in the duty-free
he's watching me, hesitant, almost
smiling. He sits on the edge of the seat,
and we talk, he's seventeen,
going to his uncle in Croydon:
"But I've got the return, like."

Last night I dreamt I was back in Dublin
trudging those empty roads again,
my German Army combat jacket
buttoned up against the wind,
fusillades of rain
sweeping the road before me.
Is he still behind me? I don't know
but I can't look back.

IX

DISPLACEMENTS

1. The Old Fort in Leiden

The square root of conquest,
and its surplus. The moon splashes down
on the stone dung of this old fort
where I plant the rhetorical flag of myself
above streets full of blonde aboriginals
their bellies bland with the food
of five continents. Ach,
my patronising absitomen
sticks in my apocalyptic craw.
Your infrastructure blinds me
but I'm too half-hearted
to damn or bless, come in
out of the cosy cold
to warm myself at your dead ash.
Evening land . . . evening land . . .
a thin German tune shafts the night
and I feel the gordian knot of twilights
and dawns, rises and falls,
like a black ball in my stomach.
It must have been something I ate.

2. Lost in Space

We cycle out into the postwar suburbs
where nothing has ever happened.
I like it here, the milky way of lives
and television sets, crammed
with roads which lead
from nowhere to nowhere –
like one which rears up now
in the suburbs of memory
lit up in the dark afternoon
by a shimmy of tinker's caravans
cruising like a runway
through the muck
of old potato fields
to end abruptly in detritus.
I played there in the ravaged woods
building fires from debris
warming myself at invisible flames
the wind tormenting their
hot red roaring heart.
I imagined myself the survivor
of some medieval battle
the derelict cars in the ditches
were slaughtered knights.
I was the last man on earth,
or maybe the first.
The rooks scour the skeletal
air of winter, clamourous ikon
sketching itself in charcoal
etching my eyes and ears.
Darkness comes loping
through the trees, like the ghost
of a barefoot gaelic army.
I ran back through the rain
till I hit the concrete
and kept on running, homing
in on five o'clock and my favourite
programme: Lost In Space.

3. *Homage*

Home in the concrete igloo, silence
seeps out of the dead TV.
Upstairs, a pageant of dead languages
words deafening each other
till one by one they fell silent
into the long night of the book.
I taken down Kuno Meyer, old technologist
of displacements, dust green parrot
stamped in gold, and read
that great ninth-century poem
of the warrior's tryst after death,
how he stands there on the riverbank
and asks: 'What is this place?'
None may address him.
His mind is gapped with purple,
pain blurs his reception
the world comes and goes,
dis-located. And I am found.
My life is here, in this moment's mirror
this capsule shooting through time
with myself, the good doctor,
and the dead warrior, locked together
by a dialectical accident
a twisted crystal which flickers
on the screen of language
a salmon that leaps
from the darkest river.

WOLFE TONE

In the dunes at Texel
an old tune raddles the air
but I'm the only one who hears it.

I am becalmed.
The day hangs slack
as a sail without wind.

A shout in the hills,
drums in the narrow streets –
a native land.

And what if I were to find it
and look upon it
as if it were the coast of Japan?

UMLAUT
George Trakl d. 1915
Francis Ledwidge d. 1917

Dreaming at my desk, I've built
this fantasy round Georg Trakl,
which seems to satisfy something,
somewhere. It's partly based
on a tale my mother told me
or maybe something I read
one schoolbagged afternoon
in the Banba Second-hand Bookshop.
It takes place in Navan,
that rivered and mirrored town,
on a day in 1917.

Matt McGoona, Meath Chronicler,
heard his friend's boneshaker
rattling into the Square.

He ran to the window, but it was empty.
In Flanders, Francis Ledwidge's bones
shook in the air.

Then a figure appears
on the banks of the Boyne,
Between Navan and Slane.
His quicklime head burns the air
his uniform is the colour
of a soiled dove. He sings,
and a passerby hears, in Beauparc,
the blackbirds's umlaut.

THE IRONY OF AMERICA

1.
I'm so far from here. Out
of the forest's familiar speakers
an African symphony blares. For days,
we thought we heard the telephone ring,
but no, no one was calling us,
not even that bird. Nor was he calling
the others, on whose lawns and buildings
a siege of flags proclaims:
we are here.

2.
New York is peopled from European novels.
Late last night we brushed past
a group of red-faced Poles, shirts open
to the cold air. They could have been
my Navan uncles, gilded youth
of an emptying village
off to a dance in 1960, smelling
of drink and soap. On one side
of the street, Perzynski's travel agency,
on the other a row of funeral parlors
like airport departure gates
sailing East.

3.
We saw him outside the Ukrainian Church,
a blond, bearded, woodcut giant
muttering to himself, lurching
in huge broken shoes his human steps.
He should have been a Holy Fool,
but he's on the wrong planet:
his suit is in shreds, his torso
naked as an unwound mummy. Here,
there is no redemption,
when stumbling, with all
the gravity of America he falls.

4.
In the early years of this century
Samuel Goldwyn, begetter of dreams
lodged in the Rotterdam lodging house
belonging to Abram Tuschinski,
both of the them part of a wagon train
scattering West. Tuschinski stayed,
to build a caravanserai
of dreams, still standing,
though he himself, like Perec's mother
was shipped back East to die.
Sam Goldwyn embarked for America:
watching their figures shrink
on the pier, he waved
and shouted: 'Bon Voyage!'

X

TO A CHILD IN THE WOMB

Little Brendan, snug in your coracle
you are right to be sailing west
to surrender your tonsured head
to the wave's harsh lick.

Your clerks have copied our manuscripts
in every one of your cells
decorated with birds and beasts
such as you'll see in the New World.

Here in the old country
the Dark Ages are always beginning
and the light that was in Troy
falls on empty motorways.

We are standing on the shore
our feet sinking into the earth.
We raise our hands to bid farewell
to catch you when you fall

over the world's edge.

BIRTH CERTIFICATE: AMSTERDAM, 22 JUNE 1988

1944: I hate those barbed-wire numbers
evil crystals breaking the light,
death's rusted formula.

Two broken crosses.
The clawprints of a monstrous bird
gouged in a century come to grief.

There is no road. Our bodies
are flimsy bridges
across the unspeakable river,

and out in to these bloodswept streets
we will carry you, alone.

Yet this year of your birth
has a pleasing shape:
two annealing eights

like the brief eclipse
of bodies when
your flesh was made flesh.

Though I know it solves nothing
though I know
it salves nothing

you have been born.
Saar, I carve your name
on the dawn

and the diamond ratchet
of your small song
turns the wheel another inch.

ICELAND

My pale daughter runs in the wind
which reminds us that this is North.
No patriot could love his fatherland
as she loves this playground
where I hear her shout in a language
I forget in my dreams.

Now, more than ever, she looks
like a child from an Icelandic saga
the foster-child, concubine's daughter
booty of war undeclared
and merely economic

This January is too cold for tourists.
Like the ghosts of themselves the canal captains
grip the wheels of motionless boats
and Vermeer's "radiant pigments"
Drown behind their diked eyes.

Daughter, I wish you islands
rising like equations
from the ocean of your life
where people rush down to the shore
to gather you into themselves
shrieking in the tongue
you did not believe existed.

MICHAEL O'LOUGHLIN was born in Dublin in 1958, and graduated from Trinity College Dublin. He has published three collections of poetry and many essays. He has received bursaries from the Irish Arts Council in 1982, 1984 and 1987 and in 1989 was resident poet at the Frost Place, New Hampshire, U.S.A. He has translated poetry from a number of languages, and published a book of short fictions, *The Inside Story*, in 1989. His poetry has appeared in such anthologies as *The Penguin Book of Contemporary Irish Poetry* and T*he Field Day Anthology of Irish Literature*, and his fiction in *The Picador Book of Contemporary Irish Fiction*. He currently lives in Amsterdam with his wife and daughter.